This edition published by Parragon Books Ltd in 2017 and distributed by

Parragon Inc.
440 Park Avenue South, 13th Floor
New York, NY 10016
www.parragon.com

ISBN 978-1-4748-9127-1

Printed in China

Disney
MINNIE

Where's Fifi?

PaRRagon
Bath · New York · Cologne · Melbourne · Delhi
Hong Kong · Shenzhen · Singapore

One sunny day, Minnie Mouse was walking her dog, Fifi, when she noticed a sign posted on a fence.

"Look, Fifi, a dog show!" Minnie said. "There are prizes, too. Fifi, I think you should enter!"

DOG SHOW!
THIS SATURDAY AT NOON
IN THE PARK

PRIZES!

The two of them raced home to practice their tricks. The show was only two days away.

As they practiced, Minnie grew more and more confident. There was no doubt about it. Fifi was one talented pup!

"Fifi, sit up," said Minnie. Fifi sat up proudly. "Now, shake my hand." Fifi held up a dainty paw.

"Good girl, Fifi!" said Minnie, shaking Fifi's paw.
"Now, roll over."

Fifi sat up and let out a loud bark, *"Ruff!"*

"No, no," said Minnie. "You're supposed to bark when I say 'speak.'"

Fifi rolled over on her back.

"Oh dear!" said Minnie. "We've got some work to do, Fifi."

The morning of the dog show arrived. Minnie gave Fifi
a scented bath and tied a polka-dot bow in her fur.
"Now we match!" said Minnie. The two of them set off.
Fifi trotted neatly beside her, toward the town square, when …

... all of a sudden, Fifi pulled at the leash and began to race down the street.

"*Ruff! Ruff!*" Fifi barked. She'd spotted a squirrel!

Minnie tugged on the leash.
"Fifi, stop!" she cried.
But Fifi was too fast. Minnie watched in surprise as Fifi slipped right out of her collar and disappeared around the corner!
"Fifi!" Minnie called out. "Please come back!"

Minnie ran around the corner, but there was no sign of Fifi. All she found was a long, bushy tail poking out of a tin can. It was the squirrel, hiding.

"Oh, Fifi," Minnie said, gazing around. "Where are you?"

Minnie raced home, hoping to find Fifi waiting for her. But she wasn't there either. Minnie called her best friend, Daisy.

"Fifi's lost," she wailed over the phone.

"I'll be right there," said Daisy. "I'll bring Mickey, too!"

By the time Mickey and Daisy arrived, Minnie was in tears.
"Don't worry, Minnie," said Mickey. "We'll help you find her."
"That's right," Daisy agreed. "I know just what to do. Let's go!"

Daisy called the town animal shelter right away.
"I want to report a missing dog," she told them.
"Her name is Fifi. When she disappeared, she was
wearing a red polka-dot bow."

Mickey and Minnie decided to make some signs.
They gathered supplies and got right to work.

Mickey and Minnie made lots of big, bold signs.
"Let's post them all around town," suggested Mickey.
"Someone is sure to find Fifi."
"Great idea, Mickey!" said Minnie.

Minnie and her helpful friends went all around the neighborhood, calling for Fifi and posting the signs.

"Great work, everyone!" said Mickey.

"Now, let's go back to your house, Minnie," suggested Daisy. "Fifi may have found her way home."

"Thank you both for helping me," said Minnie.

"No problem. We love Fifi, too!" said Mickey.

But when they reached Minnie's house, there was
still no sign of her little dog.
"Poor Fifi," Minnie said. "Where could she be?"

Just then, Daisy had an idea. "I know! I'll send a message to all my friends, asking if they've seen Fifi," she said. "With everyone's help, I'm sure we'll find her."

"Great thinking, Daisy!" said Mickey.

"Oh, thank you," said Minnie. "You two are such good friends."

We have lost a tan-and-cream dog with a red polka-dot bow, Daisy wrote to her friends. *Please keep an eye out for her!*

Within minutes, Daisy started getting messages back.

I'll go out and look!

Poor thing. I'll keep an eye out.

Sure thing, Daisy!

Hey, Daisy! Does she look like this?

Suddenly, a picture came up on Daisy's phone. It was of a cute, little dog with a red polka-dot bow—and a big, blue ribbon. It was Fifi!

"It's Fifi! It's Fifi!" Minnie said, grabbing the dog leash. Daisy quickly sent a message back: *Yes! That's Fifi! Where is she?*

When the answer came, Daisy read the reply. "She's at the dog show!" she said, her eyes lighting up. Their plan had worked. Daisy's friend had found Fifi. Minnie raced toward the park with Mickey and Daisy right behind her.

"Ruff! Ruff!" barked Fifi happily when she saw Minnie.

"Oh, Fifi, I was so worried about you!" said Minnie. "How did you get here? And how did you win a blue ribbon?"

One of the judges came over to explain. "Your dog arrived just as we began judging," he said. "Every time someone said 'sit,' your dog sat. Every time someone said 'shake,' your dog held up one of her paws. She deserved first place!"

Minnie smiled. "You clever little dog," she said.
"You're lucky no one said 'roll over'!"
Fifi sat up and barked, "Ruff!"
Minnie giggled and hugged her prize-winning dog.
"Oh, Fifi, you'll always win first place with me!"

The End